This Little Piggy

Adapted by Jennifer Liberts Weinberg
from the script "Adventures in Piggy Sitting" by Robert Ramirez
Illustrated by Mike Wall

A GOLDEN BOOK · NEW YORK

randomhouse.com/kids
ISBN 978-0-7364-3234-4 (trade) — 978-0-7364-3235-1 (ebook)
Printed in the United States of America
10 9 8 7 6 5 4 3 2 1

It's a quiet day at the Bow-tique. Minnie and her friends are putting lots of beautiful bows on the shelves.

Mrs. Pig stops by the shop to say hello. Who is in her stroller?

"Ba-ba?" squeals a cute little voice.

"Baby Oinky!" cries Minnie. "He's adorable!"

"Peekaboo! I see you!" Daisy cries as she plays with the piglet.
Baby Oinky giggles. He thinks Daisy is funny!
Mrs. Pig has an idea. "I need to go to the market," she says.
"Why don't you look after the baby for me?"

"Well . . . ," Minnie begins.
"Bye! Back in a bit!" calls Mrs. Pig.
Before Minnie knows it, she's a piggysitter!

As soon as Mrs. Pig leaves, Baby Oinky starts to cry.

"Poor thing!" says Minnie. "Daisy, you calm the baby while I fix his bottle."

Daisy dangles a Bouncy Baby Bow in front of Baby Oinky, but he cries louder.

Then Daisy jingle-jangles keys
for Baby Oinky. He cries
even louder!

Cuckoo-Loca flies over the stroller and shakes a rattle.
Baby Oinky stops crying! He coos and giggles.
"Do babies love me or what?" Cuckoo-Loca says proudly.

Baby Oinky grabs Cuckoo-Loca's tail and winds it around and around. He lets go and Cuckoo-Loca zigs and zags across the room.

"AAAHHH!" cries Cuckoo-Loca.

"Gaa-haa!" laughs Baby Oinky.

Baby Oinky climbs out of his stroller and tries to catch Cuckoo-Loca.

Daisy chases after Baby Oinky. He's a fast little piggy! "Baby Oinky, come back!" she calls.

Daisy slips on a rattle and falls right into Baby Oinky's stroller! "Help!" she cries.

Baby Oinky keeps chasing Cuckoo-Loca. The tired bird rushes inside her clock to hide. All of a sudden, the clock's door opens.

"Peekaboo!" shouts Baby Oinky.

"Aaahhh!" cries Cuckoo-Loca.

Cuckoo-Loca's clock breaks, and all her things fall out of her home. She quickly flies away, but Baby Oinky chases her again. He thinks this is the funniest game ever!

Just as Daisy finally manages to climb out of the stroller . . .
Baby Oinky bumps into her and knocks her right back in!

Minnie arrives with the baby bottle and sees what a big mess one little piggy can make.

"My goodness!" cries Minnie when she finds Daisy wearing a baby bonnet.

Minnie catches up to Baby Oinky and Cuckoo-Loca.
Cuckoo-Loca is exhausted!
"Let's settle down," says Minnie. "Ready for your milk,
Oinky?"

"Let's make sure it isn't too cold," says Daisy. She tries to test the milk by shaking some drops onto her arm, but nothing comes out. She tries again.

All the milk splashes onto poor Daisy. Baby Oinky starts to cry.

"There, there, Oinky!" says Minnie, and she spots Cuckoo-Loca's violin on the floor. Minnie has an idea! "Hurry! Follow my lead!" she says to her little bird friend.

Minnie hums a soft lullaby.
Cuckoo-Loca plays along on the violin.
Baby Oinky looks sleepier and sleepier, and then . . .

. . . he falls asleep!

Daisy gently scoops up Baby Oinky and puts him in his cozy stroller.

Minnie, Daisy, and Cuckoo-Loca are so happy that Baby Oinky is finally sleeping.

Everything is quiet and peaceful at last. Mrs. Pig returns to Minnie's Bow-tique.

"How was he?" asks Mrs. Pig.

"Well . . . ," says Cuckoo-Loca.

"A perfect little angel!" Minnie says with a smile.

"Guess I'll go get that mani-pedi and catch a movie!" says Mrs. Pig as she hands her baby bag to Minnie. "I'm so glad I found my new babysitters!"